ANITA LOBEL

Nini Lost and Found

Alfred A. Knopf
New York

THIS IS A BORZOI BOOK PUBLISHED BY ALFRED A. KNOPF

Copyright © 2010 by Anita Lobel

Visit us on the Web! www.randomhouse.com/kids

Educators and librarians, for a variety of teaching tools, visit us at www.randomhouse.com/teachers

Library of Congress Cataloging-in-Publication Data
Lobel, Anita.
Nini lost and found / Anita Lobel. — 1st ed.
p. cm.
Summary: Nini cat enjoys her outdoor adventure until she ventures too far and cannot find her way home.
ISBN 978-0-375-85880-2 (trade) — ISBN 978-0-375-95880-9 (lib. bdg.)
[1. Cats—Fiction. 2. Lost and found possessions—Fiction.] I. Title.
PZ7.L7794Nip 2010
[E]—dc22
2008048721

The illustrations in this book were created using gouache and watercolor.

MANUFACTURED IN MALAYSIA
September 2010
10 9 8 7 6 5 4 3 2 1

First Edition

Random House Children's Books supports the First Amendment and celebrates the right to read.

To Billy always
&
Nini forever

One day, when the sky was very blue and the world outside was more inviting than ever,

Nini saw that the door had been left open.

She ran down the stairs.

Out onto the deck.

Into the garden.

Away from the house, Nini looked back.
"It is cozy in there," she thought.

By the warm fireplace.

In the tickly yarn.

On the soft couch.

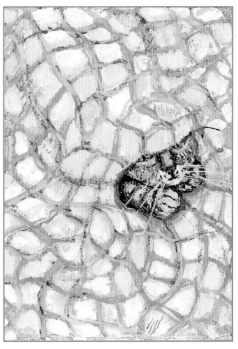

Under the big quilt.

Oh, but it was great out here.

Grasses teasing her nose.

Flowers smelling so good.

"I like it," thought Nini.

Nini walked on. Slowly at first.

Then faster.

Soon Nini had gone far away from home.
She did not look back again.

Nini roamed the woods.
What soft mosses.
What great leaves.
What good tree trunks.
And, all around, so many
interesting little creatures!
"Oh, this is really, really,
really nice," thought Nini.

But then
daylight began to fade.
Darkness began to fall.
Strange noises hovered.
Strange shapes lurked.
Nini smelled danger.

Out of the dark woods,
a big bird hooted
and flapped its wings angrily.
A slinking animal barked
and made ready to pounce.
A large, furry animal growled
and lumbered closer.

"This is not so nice anymore," thought Nini. She scooted away.

She found a hiding place.
"I can't stay here for long,"
she thought. "Those bad animals
are sure to find me."

Nini was trapped.
Nini was scared.
"I don't like it at all.
I want to go home."

It was then Nini heard, from far, far away,
the voices she knew and loved.
"Nini cat, where are you?
Where have you gone?"

"Come back, come back, little miss cat.

Nini cat, where are you?

Come home.

Where have you gone?"

Nini didn't know what to do.

"If I make a move,

those bad animals will find me."

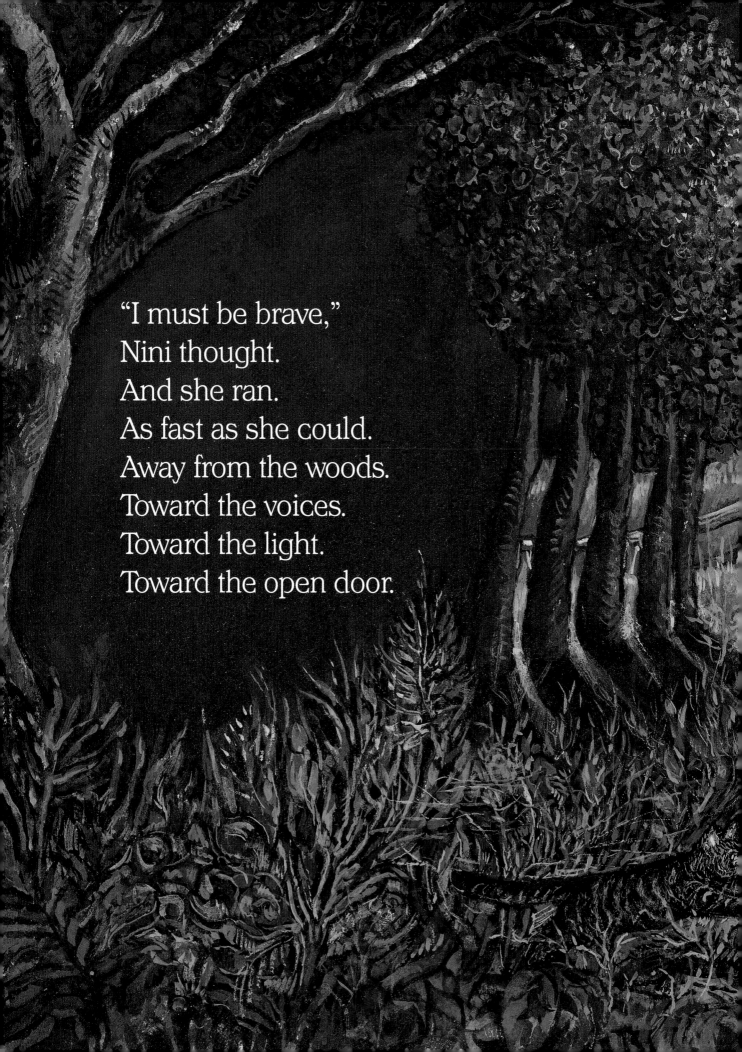

"I must be brave,"
Nini thought.
And she ran.
As fast as she could.
Away from the woods.
Toward the voices.
Toward the light.
Toward the open door.

The door closed.
Nini was home.

"You bad, bad, bad little cat. . . ."
Nini was scolded.

She meowed, meowed, meowed. . . .
The meows meant,
"I am sorry, sorry, sorry. . . ."

"We know," she was told.
"We are glad to have you back.
We love you, Nini cat."

It was good to be inside, back home.

With friendly and cozy things to hug.

And smell.

And eat.

"Out there is all right," Nini thought.
"For a little while.
But, oh, in here, at home,
is much, much, much nicer . . .

for now."